Kate Douglas Wiggin

KATE DOUGLAS WIGGIN was born Kate Smith in Philadelphia in 1856 and spent her childhood in Maine. When she was seventeen, she moved to California, where she established the first kindergarten in the West as well as a training school for teachers. In 1881 she married Samuel Wiggin, a lawyer, and moved to New York City.

A pioneer in early-childhood education, Kate Wiggin began writing children's books to raise funds for her kindergarten projects. Her first novel, *The Story of Patsy*, was published in 1883 and was followed four years later by her enormously popular *The Birds' Christmas Carol*. Of her more than twenty books, the most successful were her stories of family life, which won the author fame for her homespun humor and her understanding of children. She is best known for *Rebecca of Sunnybrook Farm*, published in 1903, and available in a Yearling Classic edition. This lively tale was one of the few girls' stories to rival Louisa May Alcott's in popularity.

Kate Douglas Wiggin died in England in 1923 shortly after completing her autobiography, *My Garden of Memory*.

Works of lasting literary merit by classic international writers

YEARLING BOOKS / YOUNG YEARLINGS / YEARLING CLASSICS are designed especially to entertain and enlighten young people. Patricia Reilly Giff, consultant to this series, received the bachelor's degree from Marymount College. She holds the master's degree in history from St. John's University, and a Professional Diploma in Reading from Hofstra University. She was a teacher and reading consultant for many years, and is the author of numerous books for young readers.

For a complete listing of all Yearling titles, write to
Dell Readers Service, P.O. Box 1045,
South Holland, IL 60473.

"The little Ruggleses bore it bravely"

The
BIRDS' CHRISTMAS CAROL

Kate Douglas Wiggin

With Illustrations

Afterword by Leon Garfield

Published by
Dell Publishing
a division of
Bantam Doubleday Dell Publishing Group, Inc.
666 Fifth Avenue
New York, New York 10103

ISBN: 0-440-40121-6

RL: 6.7

Printed in the United States of America

August 1990

12 11 10 9 8 7 6 5 4 3 2

OPM

TO THE THREE DEAREST CHILDREN
IN THE WORLD
BERTHA, LUCY, AND HORATIO

Contents
and
List of Illustrations

The
BIRDS' CHRISTMAS CAROL

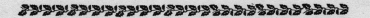

1
A Little Snow Bird

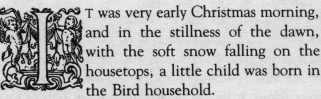T was very early Christmas morning, and in the stillness of the dawn, with the soft snow falling on the housetops, a little child was born in the Bird household.

They had intended to name the baby Lucy, if it were a girl; but they had not expected her on Christmas morning, and a real Christmas baby was not to be lightly named—the whole family agreed in that.

They were consulting about it in the nursery. Mr. Bird said that he had assisted in naming the three boys, and that he should leave this matter entirely to Mrs. Bird; Donald wanted the child

1

called "Dorothy," after a pretty, curly-haired girl who sat next him in school; Paul choose "Luella," for Luella was the nurse who had been with him during his whole babyhood, up to the time of his first trousers, and the name suggested all sorts of comfortable things. Uncle Jack said that the first girl should always be named for her mother, no matter how hideous the name happened to be.

Grandma said that she would prefer not to take any part in the discussion, and everybody suddenly remembered that Mrs. Bird had thought of naming the baby Lucy, for Grandma herself; and, while it would be indelicate for her to favor that name, it would be against human nature for her to suggest any other, under the circumstances.

Hugh, the "hitherto baby," if that is a possible term, sat in one corner and said nothing, but felt, in some mysterious way, that his nose was out of joint; for there was a newer baby now, a possibility he had never taken into consideration; and the "first girl," too,—a still higher development of treason, which made him actually green with jealousy.

2

But it was too profound a subject to be settled then and there, on the spot; besides, Mamma had not been asked, and everybody felt it rather absurd, after all, to forestall a decree that was certain to be absolutely wise, just, and perfect.

The reason that the subject had been brought up at all so early in the day lay in the fact that Mrs. Bird never allowed her babies to go over night unnamed. She was a person of so great decision of character that she would have blushed at such a thing; she said that to let blessed babies go dangling and dawdling about without names, for months and months, was enough to ruin them for life. She also said that if one could not make up one's mind in twenty-four hours it was a sign that— But I will not repeat the rest, as it might prejudice you against the most charming woman in the world.

So Donald took his new velocipede and went out to ride up and down the stone pavement and notch the shins of innocent people as they passed by, while Paul spun his musical top on the front steps.

But Hugh refused to leave the scene of action. He seated himself on the top stair in the hall, banged his head against the railing a few times, just by way of uncorking the vials of his wrath, and then subsided into gloomy silence, waiting to declare war if more "first girl babies" were thrust upon a family already surfeited with that unnecessary article.

Meanwhile dear Mrs. Bird lay in her room, weak, but safe and happy, with her sweet girl baby by her side and the heaven of motherhood opening again before her. Nurse was making gruel in the kitchen, and the room was dim and quiet. There was a cheerful open fire in the grate, but though the shutters were closed, the side windows that looked out on the Church of Our Saviour, next door, were a little open.

Suddenly a sound of music poured out into the bright air and drifted into the chamber. It was the boy choir singing Christmas anthems. Higher and higher rose the clear, fresh voices, full of hope and cheer, as children's voices always are. Fuller and fuller grew the burst of melody as one glad strain fell upon another in joyful harmony:—

> "Carol, brothers, carol,
>   Carol joyfully,
>   Carol the good tidings,
>   Carol merrily!
>   And pray a gladsome Christmas
>   For all your fellow-men:
>   Carol, brothers, carol,
>   Christmas Day again."

One verse followed another, always with the same sweet refrain:—

> "And pray a gladsome Christmas
>   For all your fellow-men:
>   Carol, brothers, carol,
>   Christmas Day again."

Mrs. Bird thought, as the music floated in upon her gentle sleep, that she had slipped into heaven with her new baby, and that the angels were bidding them welcome. But the tiny bundle by her side stirred a little, and though it was scarcely more than the ruffling of a feather, she awoke; for the mother-ear is so close to the heart that it can hear the faintest whisper of a child.

She opened her eyes and drew the baby closer. It looked like a rose dipped in milk, she thought, this pink and white blossom of girlhood, or like a pink cherub, with its halo of pale yellow hair, finer than floss silk.

> "Carol, brothers, carol,
> Carol joyfully,
> Carol the good tidings,
> Carol merrily!"

The voices were brimming over with joy.

"Why, my baby," whispered Mrs. Bird in soft surprise, "I had forgotten what day it was. You are a little Christmas child, and we will name you 'Carol' —mother's Christmas Carol!"

"What!" said Mr. Bird, coming in softly and closing the door behind him.

"Why, Donald, don't you think 'Carol' is a sweet name for a Christmas baby? It came to me just a moment ago in the singing, as I was lying here half asleep and half awake."

"I think it is a charming name, dear heart, and sounds just like you, and I hope that, being a girl, this baby has some chance of being as lovely as her mother;"—at which speech from the baby's papa, Mrs. Bird, though she was as weak and tired as she could be, blushed with happiness.

And so Carol came by her name.

Of course, it was thought foolish by many people, though Uncle Jack declared laughingly that it was very strange if a whole family of Birds could not be indulged in a single Carol; and Grandma, who adored the child, thought the name much more appropriate than Lucy, but was glad that people would probably think it short for Caroline.

Perhaps because she was born in holiday time, Carol was a very happy baby. Of course, she was too tiny to understand the joy of Christmas-tide,

"She is a little Christmas child"

but people say there is everything in a good beginning, and she may have breathed in unconsciously the fragrance of evergreens and holiday dinners; while the peals of sleigh-bells and the laughter of happy children may have fallen upon her baby ears and wakened in them a glad surprise at the merry world she had come to live in.

Her cheeks and lips were as red as hollyberries; her hair was for all the world the color of a Christmas candle-flame; her eyes were bright as stars; her laugh like a chime of Christmasbells, and her tiny hands forever outstretched in giving.

Such a generous little creature you never saw! A spoonful of bread and milk had always to be taken by Mamma or nurse before Carol could enjoy her supper; whatever bit of cake or sweetmeat found its way into her pretty fingers was straightway broken in half to be shared with Donald, Paul, or Hugh; and when they made believe nibble the morsel with affected enjoyment, she would clap her hands and crow with delight.

"Why does she do it?" asked Donald thoughtfully. "None of us boys ever did."

"I hardly know," said Mamma, catching her darling to her heart, "except that she is a little Christmas child, and so she has a tiny share of the blessedest birthday the world ever knew!"

2

Drooping Wings

T was December, ten years later.

Carol had seen nine Christmas trees lighted on her birthdays, one after another; nine times she had assisted in the holiday festivities of the household, though in her babyhood her share of the gayeties was somewhat limited.

For five years, certainly, she had hidden presents for Mamma and Papa in their own bureau drawers, and harbored a number of secrets sufficiently large to burst a baby brain, had it not been for the relief gained by whispering them all to Mamma, at night, when she was in her crib, a proceeding which did not in the least lessen the value of a secret in her innocent mind.

For five years she had heard " 'Twas the night before Christmas," and hung up a scarlet stocking many sizes too large for her, and pinned a sprig of holly on her little white nightgown, to show Santa Claus that she was a "truly" Christmas child, and dreamed of fur-coated saints and toy-packs and reindeer, and wished everybody a "Merry Christmas" before it was light in the morning, and lent every one of her new toys to the neighbors' children before noon, and eaten turkey and plum-pudding, and gone to bed at night in a trance of happiness at the day's pleasures.

Donald was away at college now. Paul and Hugh were great manly fellows, taller than their mother. Papa Bird had gray hairs in his whiskers; and Grandma, God bless her, had been four Christmases in heaven.

But Christmas in the Birds' Nest was scarcely as merry now as it used to be in the bygone years, for the little child, that once brought such an added blessing to the day, lay month after month a patient, helpless invalid, in the room where she was born. She had never been very strong in body, and it was with a pang of terror her mother and father noticed, soon after she was five years old, that she began to limp, ever so slightly; to complain too often of weariness, and to nestle close to her mother, saying she "would rather not go out to play, please." The illness was slight at first, and hope was always stirring in Mrs. Bird's heart. "Carol would feel stronger in the summer-time;" or, "She would be better when she had spent a year in the country;" or, "She would outgrow it;" or, "They would try a new physician;" but by and by it came to be all too sure that no physician save One could make Carol strong again, and that no "summer-time" nor "country air," unless it were the everlasting summer-time in a heavenly country, could bring back the little girl to health.

The cheeks and lips that were once as red as holly-berries faded to faint pink; the star-like eyes grew softer, for they often gleamed through

13

tears; and the gay child-laugh, that had been like a chime of Christmas bells, gave place to a smile so lovely, so touching, so tender and patient, that it filled every corner of the house with a gentle radiance that might have come from the face of the Christ-child himself.

Love could do nothing; and when we have said that we have said all, for it is stronger than anything else in the whole wide world. Mr. and Mrs. Bird were talking it over one evening, when all the children were asleep. A famous physician had visited them that day, and told them that some time, it might be in one year, it might be in more, Carol would slip quietly off into heaven, whence she came.

"It is no use to close our eyes to it any longer," said Mr. Bird, as he paced up and down the library floor; "Carol will never be well again. It almost seems as if I could not bear it when I think of that loveliest child doomed to lie there day after day, and, what is still more, to suffer pain that we are helpless to keep away from her. Merry Christmas, indeed; it gets to be the sad-

dest day in the year to me!" and poor Mr. Bird
sank into a chair by the table, and buried his
face in his hands to keep his wife from seeing
the tears that would come in spite of all his
efforts.

"But, Donald, dear," said sweet Mrs. Bird,
with trembling voice, "Christmas Day may not
be so merry with us as it used, but it is very
happy, and that is better, and very blessed, and
that is better yet. I suffer chiefly for Carol's sake,
but I have almost given up being sorrowful for
my own. I am too happy in the child, and I see
too clearly what she has done for us and the
other children. Donald and Paul and Hugh were
three strong, willful, boisterous boys, but now
you seldom see such tenderness, devotion, thought
for others, and self-denial in lads of their years.
A quarrel or a hot word is almost unknown in
this house, and why? Carol would hear it, and it
would distress her, she is so full of love and
goodness. The boys study with all their might
and main. Why? Partly, at least, because they
like to teach Carol, and amuse her by telling her

what they read. When the seamstress comes, she likes to sew in Miss Carol's room, because there she forgets her own troubles, which, Heaven knows, are sore enough! And as for me, Donald, I am a better woman every day for Carol's sake; I have to be her eyes, ears, feet, hands,—her strength, her hope; and she, my own little child, is my example!"

"I was wrong, dear heart," said Mr. Bird more cheerfully; "we will try not to repine, but to rejoice instead, that we have an 'angel of the house.'"

"And as for her future," Mrs. Bird went on, "I think we need not be over-anxious. I feel as if she did not belong altogether to us, but that when she has done what God sent her for, He will take her back to Himself—and it may not be very long!" Here it was poor Mrs. Bird's turn to break down, and Mr. Bird's turn to comfort her.

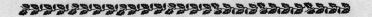

3
The Birds' Nest

AROL herself knew nothing of motherly tears and fatherly anxieties; she lived on peacefully in the room where she was born.

But you never would have known that room; for Mr. Bird had a great deal of money, and though he felt sometimes as if he wanted to throw it all in the sea, since it could not buy a strong body for his little girl, yet he was glad to make the place she lived in just as beautiful as it could be.

The room had been extended by the building of a large addition that hung out over the garden below, and was so filled with windows that it might have been a conservatory. The ones on

the side were thus still nearer the Church of Our
Saviour than they used to be; those in front
looked out on the beautiful harbor, and those in
the back commanded a view of nothing in particular but a narrow alley; nevertheless, they
were pleasantest of all to Carol, for the Ruggles
family lived in the alley, and the nine little,
middle-sized, and big Ruggles children were a
source of inexhaustible interest.

The shutters could all be opened and Carol
could take a real sun-bath in this lovely glass
house, or they could all be closed when the dear
head ached or the dear eyes were tired. The
carpet was of soft gray, with clusters of green bay
and holly leaves. The furniture was of white
wood, on which an artist had painted snow scenes
and Christmas trees and groups of merry children ringing bells and singing carols.

Donald had made a pretty, polished shelf,
and screwed it on the outside of the foot-board,
and the boys always kept this full of blooming
plants, which they changed from time to time;
the head-board, too, had a bracket on either

side, where there were pots of maiden-hair ferns.

Love-birds and canaries hung in their golden houses in the windows, and they, poor caged things, could hop as far from their wooden perches as Carol could venture from her little white bed.

On one side of the room was a bookcase filled with hundreds—yes, I mean it—with hundreds and hundreds of books; books with gay-colored pictures, books without; books with black and white outline sketches, books with none at all; books with verses, books with stories; books that made children laugh, and some, only a few, that made them cry; books with words of one syllable for tiny boys and girls, and books with words of fearful length to puzzle wise ones.

This was Carol's "Circulating Library." Every Saturday she chose ten books, jotting their names down in a diary; into these she slipped cards that said:—

"Please keep this book two weeks and read it. With love,   CAROL BIRD."

Then Mrs. Bird stepped into her carriage and

took the ten books to the Children's Hospital, and brought home ten others that she had left there the fortnight before.

This was a source of great happiness; for some of the Hospital children that were old enough to print or write, and were strong enough to do it, wrote Carol sweet little letters about the books, and she answered them, and they grew to be friends. (It is very funny, but you do not always have to see people to love them. Just think about it, and tell me if it isn't so.)

There was a high wainscoting of wood about the room, and on top of this, in a narrow gilt framework, ran a row of illuminated pictures, illustrating fairy tales, all in dull blue and gold and scarlet and silver. From the door to the closet there was the story of "The Fair One with Golden Locks;" from closet to bookcase, ran "Puss in Boots;" from bookcase to fireplace, was "Jack the Giant-killer'" and on the other side of the room were "Hop o' my Thumb," "The Sleeping Beauty," and "Cinderella."

Then there was a great closet full of beautiful

things to wear, but they were all dressing-gowns and slippers and shawls; and there were drawers full of toys and games, but they were such as you could play with on your lap. There were no ninepins, nor balls, nor bows and arrows, nor bean bags, nor tennis rackets; but, after all, other children needed these more than Carol Bird, for she was always happy and contented, whatever she had or whatever she lacked; and after the room had been made so lovely for her, on her eighth Christmas, she always called herself, in fun, a "Bird of Paradise."

On these particular December days she was happier than usual, for Uncle Jack was coming from England to spend the holidays. Dear, funny, jolly, loving, wise Uncle Jack, who came every two or three years, and brought so much joy with him that the world looked as black as a thunder-cloud for a week after he went away again.

The mail had brought this letter:—

LONDON, November 28, 188—.
Wish you merry Christmas, you dearest birdlings in America! Preen your feathers, and stretch

the Birds' nest a trifle, if you please, and let Uncle Jack in for the holidays. I am coming with such a trunk full of treasures that you'll have to borrow the stockings of Barnum's Giant and Giantess; I am coming to squeeze a certain little lady-bird until she cries for mercy; I am coming to see if I can find a boy to take care of a black pony that I bought lately. It's the strangest thing I ever knew; I've hunted all over Europe, and can't find a boy to suit me! I'll tell you why. I've set my heart on finding one with a dimple in his chin, because this pony particularly likes dimples! ["Hurrah!" cried Hugh; "bless my dear dimple; I'll never be ashamed of it again."]

Please drop a note to the clerk of the weather, and have a good, rousing snow-storm—say on the twenty-second. None of your meek, gentle, nonsensical, shilly-shallying snow-storms; not the sort where the flakes float lazily down from the sky as if they didn't care whether they ever got here or not and then melt away as soon as they touch the earth, but a regular business-like whizzing, whirring, blurring, cutting snow-storm, warranted to freeze and stay on!

I should like rather a LARGE Christmas tree, if it's convenient: not one of those "sprigs," five or six feet high, that you used to have three or four years ago, when the birdlings were not fairly feathered out; but a tree of some size. Set it up in the garret, if necessary, and then we can cut a hole in the roof if the tree chances to be too high for the room.

Tell Bridget to begin to fatten a turkey. Tell her that by the twentieth of December that turkey must not be able to stand on its legs for fat, and then on the next three days she must allow it to recline easily on its side, and stuff it to bursting. (One ounce of stuffing beforehand is worth a pound afterwards.)

The pudding must be unusually huge, and darkly, deeply, lugubriously blue in color. It must be stuck so full of plums that the pudding itself will ooze out into the pan and not be brought on to the table at all. I expect to be there by the twentieth, to manage these

23

little things myself,—remembering it is the early Bird that catches the worm,—but give you the instructions in case I should be delayed.

And Carol must decide on the size of the tree—she knows best, she was a Christmas child; and she must plead for the snow-storm—the "clerk of the weather" may pay some attention to her; and she must look up the boy with the dimple for me—she's likelier to find him than I am, this minute. She must advise about the turkey, and Bridget must bring the pudding to her bedside and let her drop every separate plum into it and stir it once for luck, or I'll not eat a single slice—for Carol is the dearest part of Christmas to Uncle Jack, and he'll have none of it without her. She is better than all the turkeys and puddings and apples and spare-ribs and wreaths and garlands and mistletoe and stockings and chimneys and sleigh-bells in Christendom! She is the very sweetest Christmas Carol that was ever written, said, sung, or chanted, and I am coming as fast as ships and railway trains can carry me, to tell her so.

24

Carol's joy knew no bounds. Mr. and Mrs. Bird laughed like children and kissed each other for sheer delight, and when the boys heard it they simply whooped like wild Indians; until the Ruggles family, whose back yard joined their garden, gathered at the door and wondered what was "up" in the big house.

Carol at her window

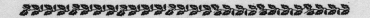

4

"Birds of a Feather Flock Together"

NCLE Jack did really come on the twentieth. He was not detained by business, nor did he get left behind nor snowed up, as frequently happens in stories, and in real life too, I am afraid. The snow-storm came also; and the turkey nearly died a natural and premature death from overeating. Donald came, too; Donald, with a line of down upon his upper lip, and Greek and Latin on his tongue, and stores of knowledge in his handsome head, and stories—bless me, you couldn't turn over a chip without reminding Donald of something that happened "at College."

One or the other was always at Carol's bedside, for they fancied her paler than she used to be, and they could not bear her out of sight. It was Uncle Jack, though, who sat beside her in the winter twilights. The room was quiet, and almost dark, save for the snow-light outside, and the flickering flame of the fire, that danced over the "Sleeping Beauty's" face and touched the Fair One's golden locks with ruddier glory. Carol's hand (all too thin and white these latter days) lay close clasped in Uncle Jack's, and they talked together quietly of many, many things.

"I want to tell you all about my plans for Christmas this year, Uncle Jack," said Carol, on the first evening of his visit, "because it will be the loveliest one I ever had. The boys laugh at me for caring so much about it; but it isn't altogether because it is Christmas, nor because it is my birthday; but long, long ago, when I first began to be ill, I used to think, the first thing when I waked on Christmas morning, 'To-day is Christ's birthday—*and mine!*' I did not put the

27

words close together, you know, because that made it seem too bold; but I first said, 'Christ's birthday,' out loud, and then, in a minute, softly to myself—*'and mine!'* 'Christ's birthday—*and mine!'* And so I do not quite feel about Christmas as other girls do. Mamma says she supposes that ever so many other children have been born on that day. I often wonder where they are, Uncle Jack, and whether it is a dear thought to them, too, or whether I am so much in bed, and so often alone, that it means more to me. Oh, I do hope that none of them are poor, or cold, or hungry; and I wish—I wish they were all as happy as I, because they are really my little brothers and sisters. Now, Uncle Jack dear, I am going to try and make somebody happy every single Christmas that I live, and this year it is to be the 'Ruggleses in the rear.' "

"That large and interesting brood of children in the little house at the end of the back garden?"

"Yes; isn't it nice to see so many together?—

28

and, Uncle Jack, why do the big families always
live in the small houses, and the small families
in the big houses? We ought to call them the
Ruggles children, of course; but Donald began
talking of them as the 'Ruggleses in the rear,'
and Papa and Mamma took it up, and now we
cannot seem to help it. The house was built for
Mr. Carter's coachman, but Mr. Carter lives in
Europe, and the gentleman who rents his place
for him doesn't care what happens to it, and so
this poor family came to live there. When they
first moved in, I used to sit in my window and
watch them play in their back yard; they are so
strong, and jolly, and good-natured;—and then,
one day, I had a terrible headache, and Donald
asked them if they would please not scream quite
so loud, and they explained that they were having a game of circus, but that they would change
and play 'Deaf and Dumb Asylum' all the
afternoon."

"Ha, ha, ha!" laughed Uncle Jack, "what an
obliging family, to be sure!"

"Yes, we all thought it very funny, and I

smiled at them from the window when I was
well enough to be up again. Now, Sarah Maud
comes to her door when the children come
home from school, and if Mamma nods her
head, 'Yes,' that means 'Carol is very well,' and
then you ought to hear the little Ruggleses
yell,—I believe they try to see how much noise
they can make; but if Mamma shakes her head,
'No,' they always play at quiet games. Then, one
day, 'Cary,' my pet canary, flew out of her cage,
and Peter Ruggles caught her and brought her
back, and I had him up here in my room to
thank him."

"Is Peter the oldest?"

"No; Sarah Maud is the oldest—she helps do
the washing; and Peter is the next. He is a
dressmaker's boy."

"And which is the pretty little red-haired
girl?"

"That's Kitty."

"And the fat youngster?"

"Baby Larry."

"And that—most freckled one?"

"Now, don't laugh—that's Peoria."

"Carol, you are joking."

"No, really, Uncle dear. She was born in Peoria; that's all."

"And is the next boy Oshkosh?"

"No," laughed Carol, "the others are Susan, and Clement, and Eily, and Cornelius; they all look exactly alike, except that some of them have more freckles than the others."

"How did you ever learn all their names?"

"Why, I have what I call a 'window-school.' It is too cold now; but in warm weather I am wheeled out on my balcony, and the Ruggleses climb up and walk along our garden fence, and sit down on the roof of our carriage-house. That brings them quite near, and I tell them stories. On Thanksgiving Day they came up for a few minutes,—it was quite warm at eleven o'clock,— and we told each other what we had to be thankful for; but they gave such queer answers that Papa had to run away for fear of laughing; and I couldn't understand them very well. Susan was thankful for 'trunks,' of all things in the

31

world; Cornelius, for 'horse-cars;' Kitty, for 'pork steak;' while Clem, who is very quiet, brightened up when I came to him, and said he was thankful for *'his lame puppy.'* Wasn't that pretty?"

"It might teach some of us a lesson, mightn't it, little girl?"

"That's what Mamma said. Now I'm going to give this whole Christmas to the Ruggleses; and, Uncle Jack, I earned part of the money myself."

"You, my bird; how?"

"Well, you see, it could not be my own, own Christmas if Papa gave me all the money, and I thought to really keep Christ's birthday I ought to do something of my very own; and so I talked with Mamma. Of course she thought of something lovely; she always does: Mamma's head is just brimming over with lovely thoughts,—all I have to do is ask, and out pops the very one I want. This thought was to let her write down, just as I told her, a description of how a child lived in her own room for three years, and what

32

she did to amuse herself; and we sent it to a magazine and got twenty-five dollars for it. Just think!"

"Well, well," cried Uncle Jack, "my little girl a real author! And what are you going to do with this wonderful 'own' money of yours?"

"I shall give the nine Ruggleses a grand Christmas dinner here in this very room—that will be Papa's contribution,—and afterwards a beautiful Christmas tree, fairly blooming with presents—that will be my part; for I have another way of adding to my twenty-five dollars, so that I can buy nearly anything I choose. I should like it very much if you would sit at the head of the table, Uncle Jack, for nobody could ever be frightened of you, you dearest, dearest, dearest thing that ever was! Mamma is going to help us, but Papa and the boys are going to eat together downstairs for fear of making the little Ruggleses shy; and after we've had a merry time with the tree we can open my window and all listen together to the music at the evening church-service, if it comes before the children go. I have written a letter to the organist, and asked him if I might have the two songs I like best. Will you see if it is all right?"

BIRDS' NEST, December 21, 188—.

DEAR MR. WILKIE,—I am the little girl who lives next door to the church, and, as I seldom go out, the music on practice days and Sundays is one of my greatest pleasures.

I want to know if you can have "Carol, brothers, carol," on Christmas night, and if the boy who sings "My ain countree" so beautifully may please sing that too. I think it is the loveliest thing in the world, but it always makes me cry; doesn't it you?

If it isn't too much trouble, I hope they can sing them both quite early, as after ten o'clock I may be asleep.

Yours respectfully,
CAROL BIRD

P.S.—The reason I like "Carol, brothers, carol," is because the choir-boys sang it eleven years ago, the morning I was born, and put it into Mamma's head to call me Carol. She didn't remember then that my other name would be Bird, because she was half asleep, and could only think of one thing at a time. Donald says if I had been born on the Fourth of July they would have named me "Independence," or if on the twenty-second of February, "Georgina," or even "Cherry," like Cherry in "Martin Chuzzlewit;" but I like my own name and birthday best.

Yours truly,
CAROL BIRD

Uncle Jack thought the letter quite right, and did not even smile at her telling the organist so many family items.

The days flew by as they always fly in holiday time, and it was Christmas Eve before anybody knew it. The family festival was quiet and very

35

pleasant, but almost overshadowed by the grander preparations for the next day. Carol and Elfrida, her pretty German nurse, had ransacked books, and introduced so many plans, and plays, and customs, and merry-makings from Germany, and Holland, and England, and a dozen other countries, that you would scarcely have known how or where you were keeping Christmas. Even the dog and the cat had enjoyed their celebration under Carol's direction. Each had a tiny table with a lighted candle in the centre, and a bit of Bologna sausage placed very near it; and everybody laughed till the tears stood in their eyes to see Villikins and Dinah struggle to nibble the sausages, and at the same time to evade the candle flame. Villikins barked, and sniffed, and howled in impatience, and after many vain attempts succeeded in dragging off the prize, though he singed his nose in doing it. Dinah, meanwhile, watched him placidly, her delicate nostrils quivering with expectation, and, after all excitement had subsided, walked with dignity to the table, her beautiful gray satin

36

tail sweeping behind her, and, calmly putting up one velvet paw, drew the sausage gently down, and walked out of the room without turning a hair, so to speak. Elfrida had scattered handfuls of seed over the snow in the garden, that the wild birds might have a comfortable breakfast next morning, and had stuffed bundles of dry grasses in the fireplaces, so that the reindeer of Santa Claus could refresh themselves after their long gallops across country. This was really only done for fun, but it pleased Carol.

And when, after dinner, the whole family had gone to the church to see the Christmas decorations, Carol limped out on her slender crutches, and with Elfrida's help, placed all the family boots in a row in the upper hall. That was to keep the dear ones from quarreling all through the year. There were Papa's stout top boots; Mamma's pretty buttoned shoes next; then Uncle Jack's, Donald's, Paul's, and Hugh's; and at the end of the line her own little white worsted slippers. Last, and sweetest of all, like the children in Austria, she put a lighted candle in her window to guide the dear Christ-child, lest he should stumble in the dark night as he passed up the deserted street. This done, she dropped into bed, a rather tired, but very happy Christmas fairy.

The "Window School"

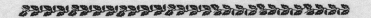

5

Some Other Birds are Taught to Fly

EFORE the earliest Ruggles could wake and toot his five-cent tin horn, Mrs. Ruggles was up and stirring about the house, for it was a gala day in the family. Gala day! I should think so! Were not her nine "childern" invited to a dinner-party at the great house, and weren't they going to sit down free and equal with the mightiest in the land? She had been preparing for this grand occasion ever since the receipt of Carol Bird's invitation, which, by the way, had been speedily enshrined in an old photograph frame and hung under the looking-glass in the most prominent place in the kitchen, where it stared the occasional visitor directly in the eye, and made him livid with envy:—

BIRDS' NEST, December 17, 188—.

DEAR MRS. RUGGLES,—I am going to have a dinner-party on Christmas Day, and would like to have all your children come. I want them every one, please, from Sarah Maud to Baby Larry. Mamma says dinner will be at half past five, and the Christmas tree at seven; so you may expect them home at nine o'clock. Wishing you a Merry Christmas and a Happy New Year, I am

Yours truly,
CAROL BIRD

Breakfast was on the table promptly at seven o'clock, and there was very little of it, too; for it was an excellent day for short rations, though Mrs. Ruggles heaved a sigh as she reflected that the boys, with their India-rubber stomachs, would be just as hungry the day after the dinner-party as if they had never had any at all.

As soon as the scanty meal was over, she announced the plan of the campaign: "Now, Susan, you an' Kitty wash up the dishes; an' Peter, can't yer spread up the beds, so 't I can git ter cuttin' out Larry's new suit? I ain't satisfied with his clo'es, an' I thought in the night of a way to make him a dress out o' my old red plaid shawl—kind o' Scotch style, yer know, with the fringe 't the bottom.—Eily, you go find the comb and take the snarls out the fringe, that's a lady! You little young ones clear out from under foot! Clem, you and Con hop into bed with Larry while I wash yer underflannins; 't won't take long to dry 'em.—Yes, I know it's bothersome, but yer can't go int' s'ciety 'thout takin' some trouble, 'n' anyhow I couldn't git round to 'em last night.—Sarah Maud, I think 't would be perfeckly han'som' if you ripped them brass buttons off yer uncle's *p*oliceman's coat 'n' sewed 'em in a row up the front o' yer green skirt. Susan, you must iron out yours 'n' Kitty's apurns;

41

'n' there, I come mighty near forgettin' Peory's stockin's! I counted the whole lot last night when I was washin' of 'em, 'n' there ain't but nineteen anyhow yer fix 'em, 'n' no nine pairs mates nohow; 'n' I ain't goin' ter have my childern wear odd stockin's to a dinner-comp'ny, fetched up as I was!—Eily, can't you run out and ask Mis' Cullen ter lend me a pair o' stockin's for Peory, 'n' tell her if she will, Peory'll give Jim half her candy when she gets home. Won't yer, Peory?"

Peoria was young and greedy, and thought the remedy so out of all proportion to the disease, that she set up a deafening howl at the projected bargain—a howl so rebellious and so entirely out of season that her mother started in her direction with flashing eye and uplifted hand; but she let it fall suddenly, saying, "No, I vow I won't lick ye Christmas Day, if yer drive me crazy; but speak up smart, now, 'n' say whether yer'd ruther give Jim Cullen half yer candy or go bare-legged ter the party?" The matter being put so plainly, Peoria collected her faculties, dried her tears,

42

and chose the lesser evil, Clem having hastened the decision by an affectionate wink, that meant he'd go halves with her on his candy.

"That's a lady!" cried her mother. "Now, you young ones that ain't doin' nothin', play all yer want ter before noontime, for after ye git through eatin' at twelve o'clock me 'n' Sarah Maud's goin' ter give yer sech a washin' 'n' combin' 'n' dressin' as yer never had before 'n' never will agin likely, 'n' then I'm goin' to set yer down 'n' give yer two solid hours trainin' in manners; 'n' 'twon't be no foolin' neither."

"All we've got ter do's go eat!" grumbled Peter.

"Well, that's enough," responded his mother; "there's more'n one way of eatin', let me tell yer, 'n' you've got a heap ter learn about it, Peter Ruggles. Land sakes, I wish you childern could see the way I was fetched up to eat. I never took a meal o' vittles in the kitchen before I married Ruggles; but yer can't keep up that style with nine young ones 'n' yer Pa always off ter sea."

The big Ruggleses worked so well, and the little Ruggleses kept from "under foot" so suc-

cessfully, that by one o'clock nine complete toi-
lets were laid out in solemn grandeur on the
beds. I say, "complete;" but I do not know
whether they would be called so in the best
society. The law of compensation had been well
applied: he that had necktie had no cuffs; she
that had sash had no handkerchief, and *vice
versa;* but they all had shoes and a certain amount
of clothing, such as it was, the outside layer
being in every case quite above criticism.

"Now, Sarah Maud," said Mrs. Ruggles, her
face shining with excitement, "everything's red
up an' we can begin. I've got a boiler 'n' a kettle
'n' a pot o' hot water. Peter, you go into the
back bedroom, 'n' I'll take Susan, Kitty, Peory,
'n' Cornelius; 'n' Sarah Maud, you take Clem,
'n' Eily, 'n' Larry, one to a time. Scrub 'em 'n'
rinse 'em, or, 't any rate git's fur's yer can with
'em, and then I'll finish 'em off while you do
yerself."

Sarah Maud couldn't have scrubbed with any
more decision and force if she had been doing
floors, and the little Ruggleses bore it bravely,

not from natural heroism, but for the joy that was set before them. Not being satisfied, however, with the "tone" of their complexions, and feeling that the number of freckles to the square inch was too many to be tolerated in the highest social circles, she wound up operations by applying a little Bristol brick from the knife-board, which served as the proverbial "last straw," from under which the little Ruggleses issued rather red and raw and out of temper. When the clock struck four they were all clothed, and most of them in their right minds, ready for those last touches that always take the most time.

Kitty's red hair was curled in thirty-four ringlets, Sarah Maud's was braided in one pig-tail, and Susan's and Eily's in two braids apiece, while Peoria's resisted all advances in the shape of hair oils and stuck out straight on all sides, like that of the Circassian girl of the circus—so Clem said; and he was sent into the bedroom for it, too, from whence he was dragged out forgivingly, by Peoria herself, five minutes later. Then, exciting moment, came linen collars for some

and neckties and bows for others,—a magnificent green glass breastpin was sewed into Peter's
purple necktie,—and Eureka! the Ruggleses were
dressed, and Solomon in all his glory was not
arrayed like one of these!

A row of seats was then formed directly through
the middle of the kitchen. Of course, there were
not quite chairs enough for ten, since the family
had rarely wanted to sit down all at once, somebody always being out or in bed, or otherwise
engaged, but the wood-box and the coal-hod
finished out the line nicely, and nobody thought
of grumbling. The children took their places
according to age, Sarah Maud at the head and
Larry on the coal-hod, and Mrs. Ruggles seated
herself in front, surveying them proudly as she
wiped the sweat of honest toil from her brow.

"Well," she exclaimed, "if I do say so as
shouldn't, I never see a cleaner, more stylish
mess o' childern in my life! I do wish Ruggles
could look at ye for a minute!—Larry Ruggles,
how many times have I got ter tell yer not ter
keep pullin' at yer sash? Haven't I told yer if it

comes ontied, yer waist 'n' skirt'll part comp'ny in the middle, 'n' then where'll yer be?—Now look me in the eye, all of yer! I've of'en told yer what kind of a family the McGrills was. I've got reason to be proud, goodness knows! Your uncle is on the *po*lice force o' New York city; you can take up the paper most any day an' see his name printed right out—James McGrill,—'n' I can't have my childern fetched up common, like some folks'; when they go out they've got to have clo'es, and learn to act decent! Now I want ter see how yer goin' ter behave when yer git there to-night. 'Tain't so awful easy as you think 'tis. Let's start in at the beginnin' 'n' act out the whole business. Pile into the bedroom, there, every last one o' ye, 'n' show me how yer goin' to go int' the parlor. This'll be the parlor, 'n' I'll be Mis' Bird."

The youngsters hustled into the next room in high glee, and Mrs. Ruggles drew herself up in the chair with an infinitely haughty and purse-proud expression that much better suited a descendant of the McGrills than modest Mrs. Bird.

47

"I want ter see how yer goin' ter behave"

The bedroom was small, and there presently ensued such a clatter that you would have thought a herd of wild cattle had broken loose. The door opened, and they straggled in, all the younger ones giggling, with Sarah Maud at the head, looking as if she had been caught in the act of stealing sheep; while Larry, being last in line, seemed to think the door a sort of gate of heaven which would be shut in his face if he didn't get there in time; accordingly he struggled ahead of his elders and disgraced himself by tumbling in head foremost.

Mrs. Ruggles looked severe. "There, I knew yer'd do it in some sech fool way! Now go in there and try it over again, every last one o' ye, 'n' if Larry can't come in on two legs he can stay ter home,—d' yer hear?"

The matter began to assume a graver aspect; the little Ruggleses stopped giggling and backed into the bedroom, issuing presently with lock step, Indian file, a scared and hunted expression on every countenance.

"No, no, no!" cried Mrs. Ruggles, in despair.

49

"That's worse yet; yer look for all the world like
a gang o' pris'ners! There ain't no style ter that:
spread out more, can't yer, 'n' act kind o'
carelesslike—nobody's goin' ter kill ye! That ain't
what a dinner-party is!"

The third time brought deserved success, and
the pupils took their seats in the row. "Now, yer
know," said Mrs. Ruggles impressively, "there
ain't enough decent hats to go round, 'n' if there
was I don' know's I'd let yer wear 'em, for the
boys would never think to take 'em off when they
got inside, for they never do—but anyhow, there
ain't enough good ones. Now, look me in the
eye. You're only goin' jest round the corner; you
needn't wear no hats, none of yer, 'n' when yer
get int' the parlor, 'n' they ask yer ter lay off yer
hats, Sarah Maud must speak up 'n' say it was
sech a pleasant evenin' 'n' sech a short walk that
yer left yer hats to home. Now, can yer remember?"

All the little Ruggleses shouted, "Yes, marm!"
in chorus.

"What have *you* got ter do with it?" demanded

their mother; "did I tell *you* to say it? Warn't I talkin' ter Sarah Maud?"

The little Ruggleses hung their diminished heads. "Yes, marm," they piped, more discreetly.

"Now we won't leave nothin' to chance; git up, all of ye, an' try it.—Speak up, Sarah Maud."

Sarah Maud's tongue clove to the roof of her mouth.

"Quick!"

"Ma thought—it was—sech a pleasant hat that we'd—we'd better leave our short walk to home," recited Sarah Maud, in an agony of mental effort.

This was too much for the boys. An earthquake of suppressed giggles swept all along the line.

"Oh, whatever shall I do with yer?" moaned the unhappy mother; "I s'pose I've got to learn it to yer!"—which she did, word for word, until Sarah Maud thought she could stand on her head and say it backwards.

"Now, Cornelius, what are *you* goin' ter say ter make yerself good comp'ny?"

"Do? Me? Dunno!" said Cornelius, turning pale, with unexpected responsibility.

"Well, ye ain't goin' to set there like a bump on a log 'thout sayin' a word ter pay for yer vittles, air ye? Ask Mis' Bird how she's feelin' this evenin', or if Mr. Bird's hevin' a busy season, or how this kind o' weather agrees with him, or somethin' like that.—Now we'll make b'lieve we've got ter the dinner—that won't be so hard, 'cause yer'll have somethin' to do—it's awful bothersome to stan' round an' act stylish. —If they have napkins, Sarah Maud down to Peory may put 'em in their laps, 'n' the rest of ye can tuck 'em in yer necks. Don't eat with yer fingers—don't grab no vittles off one 'nother's plates; don't reach out for nothin', but wait till yer asked, 'n' if you never *git* asked don't git up and grab it.—Don't spill nothin' on the table-cloth, or like's not Mis' Bird'll send yer away from the table—'n' I hope she will if yer do! (Susan! keep your handkerchief in your lap where Peory can borry it if she needs it, 'n' I hope she'll know when she does need it, though I don't expect it.) Now we'll try a few things ter see how they'll go! Mr. Clement, do you eat cramb'ry sarse?"

"Bet yer life!" cried Clem, who in the excitement of the moment had not taken in the idea exactly and had mistaken this for an ordinary bosom-of-the-family question.

"Clement McGrill Ruggles, do you mean to tell me that you'd say that to a dinner-party? I'll give ye one more chance. Mr. Clement, will you take some of the cramb'ry?"

"Yes, marm, thank ye kindly, if you happen ter have any handy."

"Very good, indeed! But they won't give yer two tries to-night,—yer just remember that! —Miss Peory, do you speak for white or dark meat?"

"I ain't perticler as ter color,—anything that nobody else wants will suit me," answered Peory with her best air.

"First-rate! Nobody could speak more genteel than that. Miss Kitty, will you have hard or soft sarse with your pudden?"

"Hard or soft? Oh! A little of both, if you please, an' I'm much obliged," said Kitty, bowing with decided ease and grace; at which all the other Ruggleses pointed the finger of shame at her, and Peter *grunted* expressively, that their meaning might not be mistaken.

"You just stop your gruntin', Peter Ruggles; that warn't greedy, that was all right. I wish I could git it inter your heads that it ain't so much what yer say, as the way you say it. And don't keep starin' cross-eyed at your necktie pin, or I'll take it out 'n' sew it on to Clem or Cornelius: Sarah Maud'll keep her eye on it, 'n' if it turns broken side out she'll tell yer. Gracious! I shouldn't think you'd ever seen nor worn no jool'ry in your life.—Eily, you an' Larry's too little to train, so you just look at the rest an' do's they do, 'n' the Lord have mercy on ye 'n' help ye to act decent! Now, is there anything more ye'd like to practice?"

"If yer tell me one more thing, I can't set up an' eat," said Peter gloomily; "I'm so cram full o' manners now I'm ready ter bust, 'thout no dinner at all."

54

"Me too," chimed in Cornelius.

"Well, I'm sorry for yer both," rejoined Mrs. Ruggles sarcastically; "if the 'mount o' manners yer've got on hand now troubles ye, you're dreadful easy hurt! Now, Sarah Maud, after dinner, about once in so often, you must git up 'n' say, 'I guess we'd better be goin',' 'n' if they say, 'Oh, no, set a while longer,' yer can set; but if they don't say nothin' you've got ter get up 'n' go. —Now hev yer got that int' yer head?"

"About once in so often!" Could any words in the language be fraught with more terrible and wearing uncertainty?

"Well," answered Sarah Maud mournfully, "seems as if this whole dinner-party set right square on top o' me! Mebbe I could manage my own manners, but to manage nine mannerses is worse'n staying to home!"

"Oh, don't fret," said her mother, good-naturedly, now that the lesson was over; "I guess you'll git along. I wouldn't mind if folks would only say, 'Oh, childern will be childern;' but they won't. They'll say, 'Land o' Goodness, who fetched them childern up?'—It's quarter past five, 'n' yer can go now:—remember 'bout the hats, —don't all talk ter once,—Susan, lend yer han'k'chief ter Peory,—Peter, don't keep screwin' yer scarf-pin,—Cornelius, hold yer head up straight,—Sarah Maud, don't take yer eyes off o' Larry, 'n' Larry you keep holt o' Sarah Maud 'n' do jest as she says,—'n' whatever you do, all of yer, never forget for one second that yer mother was a McGrill."

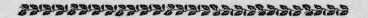

6

"When the Pie Was Opened, The Birds Began to Sing!"

THE children went out of the back door quietly, and were presently lost to sight, Sarah Maud slipping and stumbling along absent-mindedly, as she recited rapidly under her breath, "Itwassuchapleasantevenin'n'suchashortwalk, thatwethoughtwe'dleaveourhatstohome. — Itwas suchapleasantevenin'n'suchashortwalk, thatwe thoughtwe'dleaveourhatstohome."

Peter rang the door-bell, and presently a servant admitted them, and, whispering something in Sarah's ear, drew her downstairs into the kitchen. The other Ruggleses stood in horror-stricken groups as the door closed behind their commanding officer; but there was no time for reflection, for a voice from above was heard, saying, "Come right upstairs, please!"

> "Theirs not to make reply,
> Theirs not to reason why,
> Theirs but to do or die."

Accordingly they walked upstairs, and Elfrida, the nurse, ushered them into a room more splendid than anything they had ever seen. But, oh woe! where was Sarah Maud! and was it Fate that Mrs. Bird should say, at once, "Did you lay your hats in the hall?" Peter felt himself elected by circumstance the head of the family, and, casting one imploring look at tongue-tied Susan, standing next him, said huskily, "It was so very pleasant—that—that"— "That we hadn't good hats enough to go 'round," put in little Susan, bravely, to help him out, and then froze with horror that the ill-fated words had slipped off her tongue.

58

However, Mrs. Bird said, pleasantly, "Of course you wouldn't wear hats such a short distance—I forgot when I asked. Now will you come right in to Miss Carol's room? She is so anxious to see you."

Just then Sarah Maud came up the back stairs, so radiant with joy from her secret interview with the cook that Peter could have pinched her with a clear conscience; and Carol gave them a joyful welcome. "But where is Baby Larry?" she cried, looking over the group with searching eye. "Didn't he come?"

"Larry! Larry!" Good gracious, where was Larry? They were all sure that he had come in with them, for Susan remembered scolding him for tripping over the door-mat. Uncle Jack went into convulsions of laughter. "Are you sure there were nine of you?" he asked, merrily.

"I think so, sir," said Peoria, timidly; "but anyhow, there was Larry;" and she showed signs of weeping.

"Oh, well, cheer up!" cried Uncle Jack. "Probably he's not lost—only mislaid. I'll go and find him before you can say Jack Robinson!"

"I'll go, too, if you please, sir," said Sarah Maud, "for it was my place to mind him, an' if he's lost I can't relish my vittles!"

The other Ruggleses stood rooted to the floor. Was this a dinner-party, forsooth; and if so, why were such things ever spoken of as festive occasions?

Sarah Maud went out through the hall, calling, "Larry! Larry!" and without any interval of suspense a thin voice piped up from below, "Here I be!"

The truth was that Larry, being deserted by his natural guardian, dropped behind the rest, and wriggled into the hat-tree to wait for her, having no notion of walking unprotected into the jaws of a fashionable entertainment. Finding that she did not come, he tried to crawl from his refuge and call somebody, when—dark and dreadful ending to a tragic day—he found that he was too much intertwined with umbrellas and canes to move a single step. He was afraid to yell (when I have said this of Larry Ruggles I have pictured a state of helpless terror that ought to wring tears from every eye); and the sound of Sarah Maud's beloved voice, some seconds later, was like a strain of angel music in his ears. Uncle Jack dried his tears, carried him upstairs, and soon had him in breathless fits of laughter, while Carol so made the other Ruggleses forget themselves that they were presently talking like accomplished diners-out.

Carol's bed had been moved into the farthest corner of the room, and she was lying on the outside, dressed in a wonderful dressing-gown that looked like a fleecy cloud. Her golden hair fell in fluffy curls over her white forehead and neck, her cheeks flushed delicately, her eyes beamed with joy, and the children told their mother, afterwards, that she looked as beautiful as the angels in the picture books.

There was a great bustle behind a huge screen in another part of the room, and at half past five this was taken away, and the Christmas dinner-table stood revealed. What a wonderful sight it was to the poor little Ruggles children, who ate their sometimes scanty meals on the kitchen table! It blazed with tall colored candles, it gleamed with glass and silver, it blushed with flowers, it groaned with good things to eat; so it was not strange that the Ruggleses, forgetting altogether that their mother was a McGrill, shrieked in admiration of the fairy spectacle. But Larry's behavior was the most disgraceful, for he stood not upon the order of his going, but went at once for a high chair that pointed unmistakably to him, climbed up like a squirrel, gave a comprehensive look at the turkey, clapped his hands in ecstasy, rested his fat arms on the table, and cried with joy, "I beat the hull lot o' yer!" Carol laughed until she cried, giving orders, meanwhile,—"Uncle Jack, please sit at the head, Sarah Maud at the foot, and that will leave four on each side; Mamma is going to help Elfrida, so that the children need not look after each other, but just have a good time."

A sprig of holly lay by each plate, and nothing would do but each little Ruggles must leave his seat and have it pinned on by Carol, and as each course was served, one of them pleaded to take something to her. There was hurrying to and fro, I can assure you, for it is quite a difficult matter to serve a Christmas dinner on the third floor of a great city house; but if it had been necessary to carry every dish up a rope ladder the servants would gladly have done so. There were turkey and chicken, with delicious gravy and stuffing, and there were half a dozen vegetables, with cranberry jelly, and celery, and pickles; and as for the way these delicacies were served, the Ruggleses never forgot it as long as they lived.

Peter nudged Kitty, who sat next him, and said, "Look, will yer, ev'ry feller's got his own partic'lar butter; I s'pose that's to show you can eat that 'n' no more. No, it ain't either, for that pig of a Peory's just gettin' another helpin'!"

"Yes," whispered Kitty, "an' the napkins is marked with big red letters! I wonder if that's so nobody'll nip 'em; an' oh, Peter, look at the pictures stickin' right on ter the dishes! Did yer ever?"

"The Ruggleses never forgot it"

"The plums is all took out o' my cramb'ry sarse an' it's friz to a stiff jell'!" whispered Peoria, in wild excitement.

"Hi—yah! I got a wish-bone!" sang Larry, regardless of Sarah Maud's frown; after which she asked to have his seat changed, giving as excuse that he "gen'ally set beside her, an' would feel strange;" the true reason being that she desired to kick him gently, under the table, whenever he passed what might be termed "the McGrill line."

"I declare to goodness," murmured Susan, on the other side, "there's so much to look at I can't scarcely eat nothin'!"

"Bet yer life I can!" said Peter, who had kept one servant busily employed ever since he sat down; for, luckily, no one was asked by Uncle Jack whether he would have a second helping, but the dishes were quietly passed under their noses, and not a single Ruggles refused anything that was offered him, even unto the seventh time.

Then, when Carol and Uncle Jack perceived that more turkey was a physical impossibility, the meats were taken off and the dessert was brought in—a dessert that would have frightened a strong man after such a dinner as had preceded it. Not so the Ruggleses—for a strong man is nothing to a small boy—and they kindled to the dessert as if the turkey had been a dream and the six vegetables an optical delusion. There were plum-pudding, mince-pie, and ice-cream; and there were nuts, and raisins, and oranges. Kitty chose ice-cream, explaining that she knew it "by sight," though she "hadn't never tasted none;" but all the rest took the entire variety, without any regard to consequences.

"My dear child," whispered Uncle Jack, as he took Carol an orange, "there is no doubt about the necessity of this feast, but I do advise you after this to have them twice a year, or quarterly perhaps, for the way these children eat is positively dangerous; I assure you I tremble for that terrible Peoria. I'm going to run races with her after dinner."

"Never mind," laughed Carol; "let them have enough for once; it does my heart good to see them, and they shall come oftener next year."

The feast being over, the Ruggleses lay back in their chairs languidly, like little gorged boa-constrictors, and the table was cleared in a trice. Then a door was opened into the next room, and there, in a corner facing Carol's bed, which had been wheeled as close as possible, stood the brilliantly lighted Christmas tree, glittering with gilded walnuts and tiny silver balloons, and wreathed with snowy chains of pop-corn. The presents had been bought mostly with Carol's story-money, and were selected after long con-sultations with Mrs. Bird. Each girl had a blue knitted hood, and each boy a red crocheted comforter, all made by Mamma, Carol, and Elfrida. ("Because if you buy everything, it doesn't show so much love," said Carol.) Then every girl had a pretty plaid dress of a different color, and every boy a warm coat of the right size. Here the useful presents stopped, and they were quite enough; but Carol had pleaded to give them something "for fun." "I know they need the clothes," she had said, when they were talk-ing over the matter just after Thanksgiving, "but

67

they don't care much for them, after all. Now, Papa, won't you *please* let me go without part of my presents this year, and give me the money they would cost, to buy something to amuse the Ruggleses?"

"You can have both," said Mr. Bird, promptly; "is there any need of my little girl's going without her own Christmas, I should like to know? Spend all the money you like."

"But that isn't the thing," objected Carol, nestling close to her father; "it wouldn't be mine. What is the use? Haven't I almost everything already, and am I not the happiest girl in the world this year, with Uncle Jack and Donald at home? You know very well it is more blessed to give than to receive; so why won't you let me do it? You never look half as happy when you are getting your presents as when you are giving us ours. Now, Papa, submit, or I shall have to be very firm and disagreeable with you!"

"Very well, your Highness, I surrender."

"That's a dear Papa! Now what were you going to give me? Confess!"

"A bronze figure of Santa Claus; and in the 'little round belly that shakes when he laughs like a bowlful of jelly,' is a wonderful clock—oh, you would never give it up if you could see it!"

"Nonsense," laughed Carol; "as I never have to get up to breakfast, nor go to bed, nor catch trains, I think my old clock will do very well! Now, Mamma, what were you going to give me?"

"Oh, I hadn't decided. A few more books, and a gold thimble, and a smelling-bottle, and a music-box, perhaps."

"Poor Carol," laughed the child, merrily, "she can afford to give up these lovely things, for there will still be left Uncle Jack, and Donald, and Paul, and Hugh, and Uncle Rob, and Aunt Elsie, and a dozen other people to fill her Christmas stocking!"

So Carol had her way, as she generally did; but it was usually a good way, which was fortunate, under the circumstances; and Sarah Maud had a set of Miss Alcott's books, and Peter a modest silver watch, Cornelius a tool-chest, Clement a dog-house for his lame puppy, Larry a magnificent Noah's ark, and each of the younger girls a beautiful doll.

You can well believe that everybody was very merry and very thankful. All the family, from Mr. Bird down to the cook, said that they had never seen so much happiness in the space of three hours; but it had to end, as all things do. The candles flickered and went out, the tree was left alone with its gilded ornaments, and Mrs. Bird sent the children downstairs at half past eight, thinking that Carol looked tired.

"Now, my darling, you have done quite enough for one day," said Mrs. Bird, getting Carol into her little nightgown. "I'm afraid you will feel worse to-morrow, and that would be a sad ending to such a charming evening."

"Oh, wasn't it a lovely, lovely time," sighed Carol. "From first to last, everything was just right. I shall never forget Larry's face when he looked at the turkey; nor Peter's when he saw his watch; nor that sweet, sweet Kitty's smile when she kissed her dolly; nor the tears in poor, dull Sarah Maud's eyes when she thanked me for her books; nor"—

"But we mustn't talk any longer about it to-night," said Mrs. Bird, anxiously; "you are too tired, dear."

"I am not so very tired, Mamma. I have felt well all day; not a bit of pain anywhere. Perhaps this has done me good."

"Perhaps; I hope so. There was no noise or confusion; it was just a merry time. Now, may I close the door and leave you alone, dear? Papa and I will steal in softly by and by to see if you are all right; but I think you need to be very quiet."

"Oh, I'm willing to stay by myself; but I am not sleepy yet, and I am going to hear the music, you know."

"Yes, I have opened the window a little, and put the screen in front of it, so that you won't feel the air."

"Can I have the shutters open? and won't you turn my bed, please? This morning I woke ever so early, and one bright, beautiful star shone in that eastern window. I never noticed it before, and I

71

thought of the Star in the East, that guided the wise men to the place where the baby Jesus was. Good-night, Mamma. Such a happy, happy day!"

"Good-night, my precious Christmas Carol— mother's blessed Christmas child."

"Bend your head a minute, mother dear," whispered Carol, calling her mother back. "Mamma, dear, I do think that we have kept Christ's birthday this time just as He would like it. Don't you?"

"I am sure of it," said Mrs. Bird, softly.

"I beat the hull lot o' yer!"

72

The Birdling
Flies Away

THE Ruggleses had finished a last romp in the library with Paul and Hugh, and Uncle Jack had taken them home and stayed a while to chat with Mrs. Ruggles, who opened the door for them, her face all aglow with excitement and delight. When Kitty and Clem showed her the oranges and nuts that they had kept for her, she astonished them by saying that at six o'clock Mrs. Bird had sent her in the finest dinner she had ever seen in her life; and not only that, but a piece of dress-goods that must have cost a dollar a yard if it cost a cent.

As Uncle Jack went down the rickety steps he looked back into the window for a last glimpse of the family, as the children gathered about their mother, showing their beautiful presents again and again,—and then upward to a window in the great house yonder. "A little child shall lead them," he thought. "Well, if—if anything ever happens to Carol, I will take the Ruggleses under my wing."

"Softly, Uncle Jack," whispered the boys, as he walked into the library a while later. "We are listening to the music in the church. The choir has sung 'Carol, brothers, carol,' and now we think the organist is beginning to play 'My ain countree' for Carol."

"I hope she hears it," said Mrs. Bird; "but they are very late to-night, and I dare not speak to her lest she should be asleep. It is almost ten o'clock."

The boy soprano, clad in white surplice, stood in the organ loft. The light shone full upon his crown of fair hair, and his pale face, with its

74

serious blue eyes, looked paler than usual. Perhaps it was something in the tender thrill of the voice, or in the sweet words, but there were tears in many eyes both in the church and in the great house next door.

"I am far frae my hame,
  I am weary aften whiles
For the langed-for hame-bringin',
  An' my Faether's welcome smiles;
An' I'll ne'er be fu' content,
  Until my e'en do see
The gowden gates o' heaven
  In my ain countree.

"The earth is decked wi' flow'rs,
  Mony tinted, fresh an' gay,
An' the birdies warble blythely,
  For my Faether made them sae;
But these sights an' these soun's
  Will as naething be to me,
When I hear the angels singin'
  In my ain countree.

75

"My ain countree"

76

"Like a bairn to its mither,
    A wee birdie to its nest,
I fain would be gangin' noo
    Unto my Faether's breast;
For He gathers in His arms
    Helpless, worthless lambs like me,
An' carries them Himsel'
    To his ain countree."

There were tears in many eyes, but not in Carol's. The loving heart had quietly ceased to beat, and the "wee birdie" in the great house had flown to its "home nest." Carol had fallen asleep! But as to the song, I think perhaps, I cannot say, she heard it after all!

So sad an ending to a happy day! Perhaps—to those who were left; and yet Carol's mother, even in the freshness of her grief, was glad that her darling had slipped away on the loveliest day of her life, out of its glad content, into everlasting peace.

She was glad that she had gone as she had

come, on the wings of song, when all the world was brimming over with joy; glad of every grateful smile, of every joyous burst of laughter, of every loving thought and word and deed the dear last day had brought.

Sadness reigned, it is true, in the little house behind the garden; and one day poor Sarah Maud, with a courage born of despair, threw on her hood and shawl, walked straight to a certain house a mile away, up the marble steps into good Dr. Bartol's office, falling at his feet as she cried, "Oh, sir, it was me an' our children that went to Miss Carol's last dinner-party, an' if we made her worse we can't never be happy again!" Then the kind old gentleman took her rough hand in his and told her to dry her tears, for neither she nor any of her flock had hastened Carol's flight; indeed, he said that had it not been for the strong hopes and wishes that filled her tired heart, she could not have stayed long enough to keep that last merry Christmas with her dear ones.

And so the old years, fraught with memories,

die, one after another, and the new years, bright with hopes, are born to take their places; but Carol lives again in every chime of Christmas bells that peal glad tidings, and in every Christmas anthem sung by childish voices.

"I thought of the Star in the East"

79

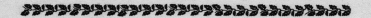

Afterword
Leon Garfield

The telephone rang. It was for my daughter, as usual. I listened. After all, I pay the bill so I have a right to know what the money's going for.

"Is that you?" asked my daughter.

"You" confessed that it was.

"Did you watch *Neighbours* last night?" *Neighbours* being an Australian soap opera of more than ordinary repulsiveness.

"You" had indeed watched it.

"Did you cry?"

"You" admitted it.

"Wasn't it sad when Peter's wife died?"

"You" said it was.

"And wasn't it awful about Sharleen?"

It was. And so it went on, the two of them exchanging sweet memories of the gorgeous tears shed in front of the television screen. There was never a word about laughter; only tears pleased them. And rightly so. As King Lear says, "The first time we smell the air, we wawl and cry. . . ." It is an ancient tradition, the tradition of the story that makes us cry. And it is not an ignoble one.

Tears, after all, are universal, while laughter is particular and often rooted in the nuances of a particular language. There is no joke that would make all the world laugh; but it is hard to imagine anyone being unmoved by, say, the death of a child.

The death of a child! The Victorians (those death-obsessed people!), loved to weep their eyes out over a dying child (while, at the same time, doing very little to prevent it!). Their books are riddled with dying children. They are planted among the pages, thick as daisies. And maybe it did some good, as the next generation certainly bestirred itself to prevent such an infantine crowding out of heaven by improving their lot upon earth.

The Birds' Christmas Carol is just one of those books; but it is a very good one. I never read it when I was young; I came to it at an age and in an age for which it was never designed. I must admit that, when I began reading it, I was taken aback by the too-sweet tenderness with which Carol—so clearly destined for heaven by the end of the book—is depicted. But even so, I found myself being deeply moved by the sincerity of it; and when I got to the

81

Ruggleses, that truly magnificent family of urchins, I was entirely captivated! I felt that Carol's brief sojourn upon earth had been worth it for the sake of meeting the Ruggleses!

I won't say that I wept when Carol was, at last, gathered up to heaven; but I can well imagine that, at a younger age, I might well have experienced a dimming of the eyes. And a good thing too! A child's tears are more valuable than its laughter. I remember Nicholas Tucker once saying that a child's sense of humor is one of its least appealing characteristics. Almost invariably, it is unkind. But a child's tears, if not for itself, show the first glimmerings of compassion. And God alone knows, that is a quality to be encouraged!

Of course, there are sentimental tales being written now, tales carefully devised to draw tears; but in general, they are not as good as *The Birds' Christmas Carol.* They are not as well-written, nor as lively, nor as sincere. Nor, do I think, will they live as long.

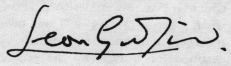